JaMeS
THE LONELY BUCK

S. J. McKeNNeY

AuthorHouse™
1663 Liberty Drive
Bloomington, IN 47403
www.authorhouse.com
Phone: 1 (833) 262-8899

Because of the dynamic nature of the Internet, any web addresses or links contained in this book may have changed
since publication and may no longer be valid. The views expressed in this work are solely those of the author and do
not necessarily reflect the views of the publisher, and the publisher hereby disclaims any responsibility for them.

Any people depicted in stock imagery provided by Getty Images are models,
and such images are being used for illustrative purposes only.
Certain stock imagery © Getty Images.

This book is printed on acid-free paper.

Interior Image Credit: Taylor D. McKenney

ISBN: 978-1-7283-7380-5 (sc)
978-1-7283-7381-2 (e)

Library of Congress Control Number: 2020917385

Print information available on the last page.

Published by AuthorHouse 09/11/2020

authorHOUSE

Presented to

Beverly,

My mom

There once was a young buck named James. He lived in a meadow, and he was all by himself in the great green forest.

James was lonely because he did not have any friends. But he really wanted one. So, James made up his mind to go out and find a friend.

One fine day, James left his home in the meadow to find that someone who would be his friend. He was walking through the forest when he heard a rustle in the bushes.

Suddenly, out of the leaves slunk Jake, the snake. Jake had big spots and a mean look on his face. He seemed to be in a hurry.

"Where are you going?" James asked nicely.

"I am looking for sssomething to eat," Jake hissed.

"May I eat with you?" asked James.

"No way!" said the snake angrily. "How dare you even assssk?"

Then Jake slithered off, and James went away lonely.

As James walked on, he almost stepped on something round in the grass. He got down on the ground and met Moe, the tortoise. Moe was very small, and very, very shy.

"What are you doing?" James asked sweetly.

"Just taking my time," Moe sighed.

"May I take my time with you?" asked James.

"Nooo," said the tortoise slowly. "I like to be alone when I take my time."

Then Moe drew his head into his shell, and James went away lonely.

The next day James left his home again and started walking. He stopped when he got to a tree that had a large bird in it. She was an eagle with colorful tail feathers, and her name was Nanny. "Why are you up there?" James asked kindly.

"I am up here so I can watch over the forest," Nanny clacked her beak.

"May I watch over the forest with you?" asked James.

"Of course not," said the eagle with a laugh. "You are a buck, and you don't have claws to perch up here like me."

Nanny waved him off with a giant wing. So, James went away lonely.

It had been a long day, but James had not lost hope. He soon came upon a busy pond in the forest. He could see a lot of bubbles in the water, and there he met Sprinkle, the goldfish. Sprinkle was famous for having the shiniest gold scales of all the goldfish in the whole pond. And she seemed very proud of that.

James knelt in the pond and politely asked, "How do you get everyone to notice you?"

"I brush my scales twice every day and swim around as fast as I can," Sprinkle glubbed.

"May I swim around with you?" asked James.

"Ew, no!" said the goldfish in a huff. "I only swim with other fish."

Then Sprinkle quickly swam away, and James went away lonely.

A little way away, James saw a duck and a swan playing together. The duck was named Harper, and the swan was named Penny. They were chasing one another back and forth.

"What are you two playing?" James asked gently.

"We are playing tag." Harper and Penny said at the same time.

"May I join your game of tag?"

"No thank you," the duck honked.

"We have enough players," the swan trumpeted.

They both paddled away, and James went away twice as lonely as before.

The next time James went in search of a friend in the forest, he found someone crying instead. It was a young doe sitting all alone.

"What is the matter?" James asked curiously.

"I am all by myself, and not one animal around here will be my friend," said the doe.

"Oh! I have been looking for a friend too. Do you want to be my friend?" asked James.

"Yes, I would love to," the doe said excitedly. "My name is Brandy. What is your name?"

"My name is James," he answered.

James and Brandy became great friends. They ate, took their time, watched over the forest, swam in the pond, and played tag together for many, many fun days.

James was never lonely again.

THe ENd

Lesson: Never give up in your search to find true friends.

About the Author

S. J. McKenney wrote this manuscript as a second grade, award winning student at Morgan Elementary School in Rialto, California. At the time she was a member of the Student Counsel, class Valedictorian, a prize winning writer of short stories, and one of the youngest participants in the Challenger Space Program for GATE students. Her favorite activities included mimicking animals, among them dogs, horses, panthers and bears. Her hobbies were reading, skating and playing video games. She most enjoyed playing with her dogs, Brutus and J. C.

-- Statement written by her dad, Michael in 1999.

S. J., as an adult currently resides in Texas. She still loves to read, write, play video games, and loves her dogs. Her mother saved this manuscript and gently requested that S. J. refresh it for other children to enjoy.